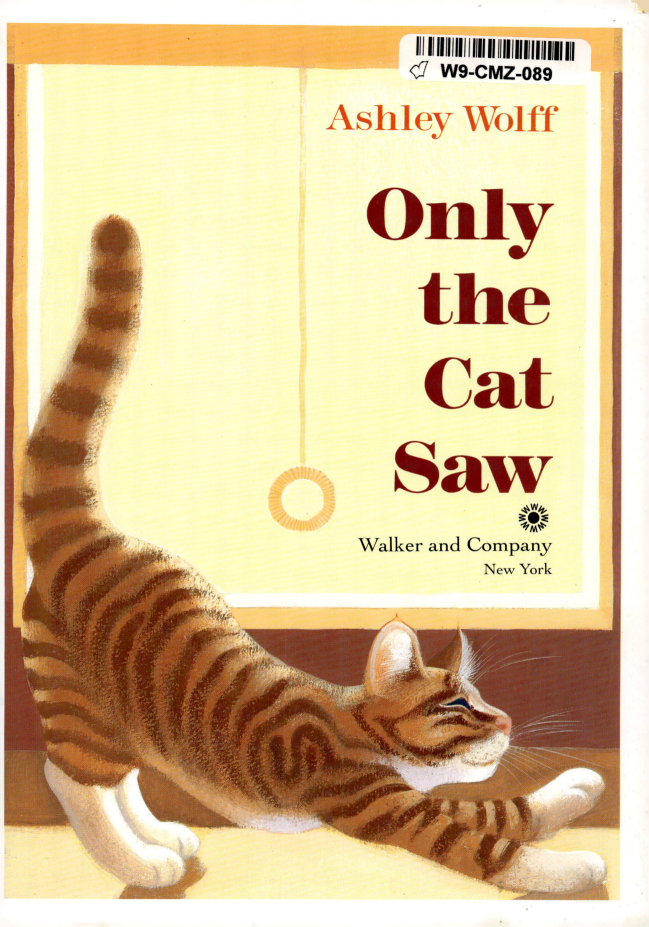

Ashley Wolff

Only the Cat Saw

Walker and Company
New York

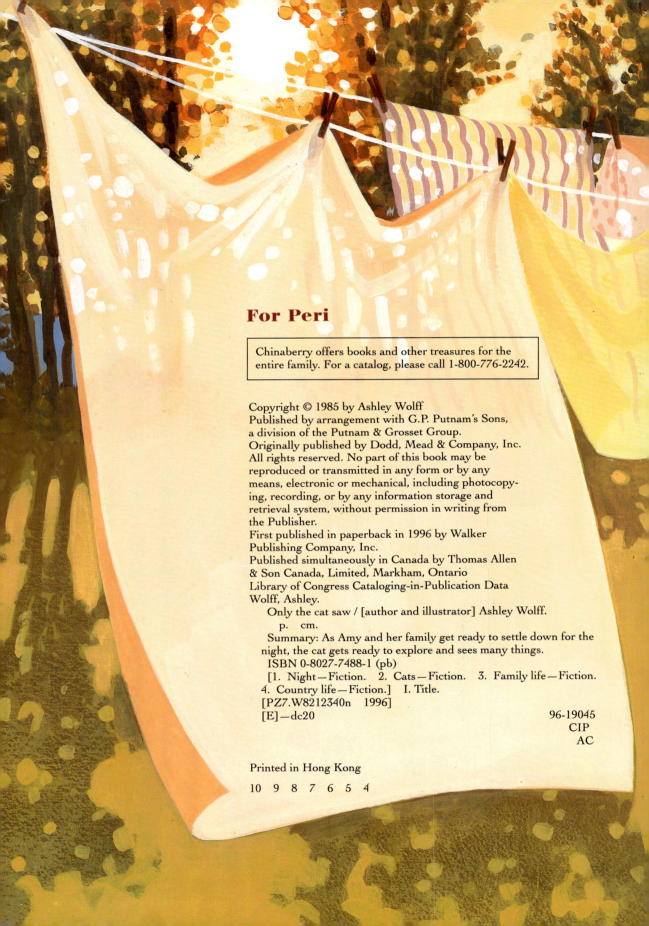

For Peri

Chinaberry offers books and other treasures for the
entire family. For a catalog, please call 1-800-776-2242.

Copyright © 1985 by Ashley Wolff
Published by arrangement with G.P. Putnam's Sons,
a division of the Putnam & Grosset Group.
Originally published by Dodd, Mead & Company, Inc.
All rights reserved. No part of this book may be
reproduced or transmitted in any form or by any
means, electronic or mechanical, including photocopy-
ing, recording, or by any information storage and
retrieval system, without permission in writing from
the Publisher.
First published in paperback in 1996 by Walker
Publishing Company, Inc.
Published simultaneously in Canada by Thomas Allen
& Son Canada, Limited, Markham, Ontario
Library of Congress Cataloging-in-Publication Data
Wolff, Ashley.
     Only the cat saw / [author and illustrator] Ashley Wolff.
        p.   cm.
     Summary: As Amy and her family get ready to settle down for the
night, the cat gets ready to explore and sees many things.
     ISBN 0-8027-7488-1 (pb)
     [1. Night—Fiction.   2. Cats—Fiction.   3. Family life—Fiction.
4. Country life—Fiction.]   I. Title.
     [PZ7.W8212340n   1996]
     [E]—dc20   96-19045
                                                                CIP
                                                                AC

Printed in Hong Kong

10 9 8 7 6 5   4

It was suppertime
and night was coming soon.
Mother was busy with Sam.
Amy was helping Father.
So only the cat saw…

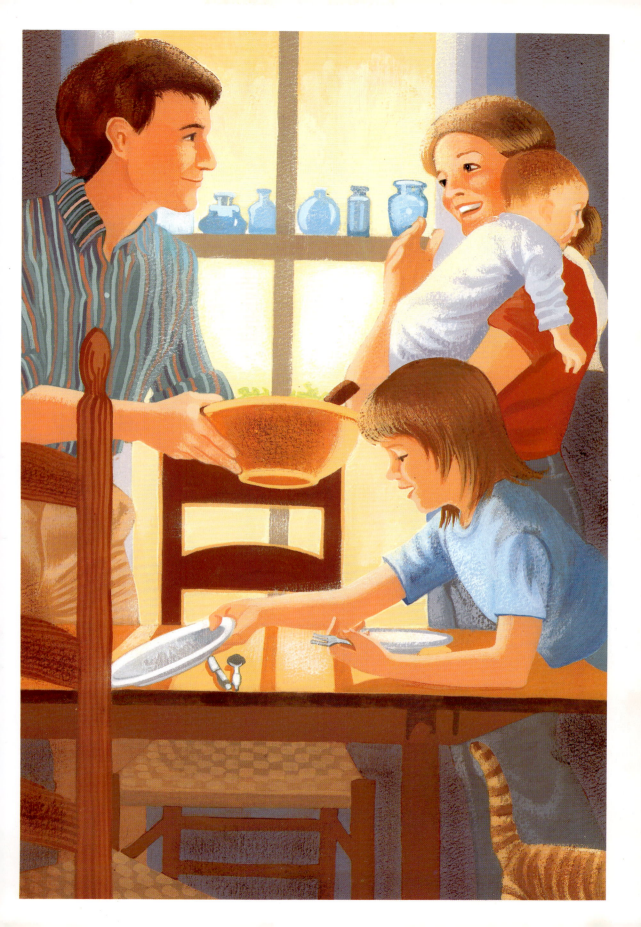

At bath time

Father was singing to Sam.

Mother was tickling Amy.

So only the cat saw…

At bedtime

Mother and Father were reading.

Sam was finally asleep, and

Amy was supposed to be.

So only the cat saw…

At midnight
Amy was dreaming.
Mother, Father, and Sam
were sleeping.
So only the cat saw...

At two o'clock in the morning
Amy got up very quietly.
No one else did.
So only the cat saw…

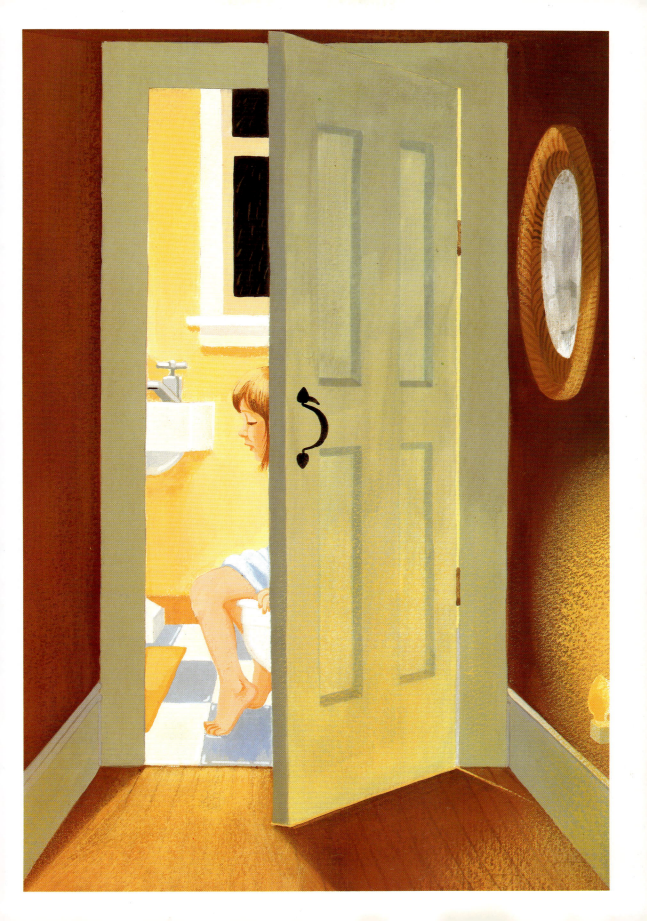

A few hours later
Sam woke Mother.
Amy and Father slept on.
So only the cat saw…

It was breakfast time,
and day had begun.
Mother was washing her face.
Sam was watching Father.
And the cat was sound asleep.
So only Amy saw…